For Samantha
Enjoy!—R.S.

Special thanks to Maria.

This book is a work of fiction. References to real people, events, or locales are intended only to provide a sense of authenticity and are used fictitiously. All other characters and all incidents and dialogue are drawn from the author's imagination and are not to be construed as real. Spike, this means you.

Scaredy-Cat, Splat!
Copyright © 2010 by Rob Scotton
All rights reserved. Printed in the United States of America.
No part of this book may be used or reproduced in any manner whatsoever without written
permission except in the case of brief quotations embodied in critical articles and reviews.
For information address HarperCollins Children's Books, a division of HarperCollins Publishers,
10 East 53rd Street, New York, NY 10022.
www.harpercollinschildrens.com

Library of Congress Cataloging-in-Publication Data
Scotton, Rob.
    Scaredy-cat, Splat! / Rob Scotton. — 1st ed.
        p. cm.
    Summary: Splat the cat accidentally succeeds in being the scariest cat in the class for Halloween.
    ISBN 978-0-06-117760-6 (trade bdg.) — ISBN 978-0-06-117761-3 (lib. bdg.)
    [1. Cats—Fiction. 2. Halloween—Fiction. 3. Costume—Fiction.] I. Title.
PZ7.S4334Sc 2010   2009049483
[E]—dc22   CIP
                                                                                                                    AC

Typography by Jeanne L. Hogle
10 11 12 13 14 LPR 10 9 8 7 6 5 4 3 2 1
❖
First Edition

Scaredy-Cat, Splat!

Rob Scotton

HARPER
An Imprint of HarperCollinsPublishers

"MOM!" cried Splat. "There's a scary spider on my jack-o'-lantern! He's small and hairy with really funny eyes."

Splat's voice wobbled with worry.

"But you're small and hairy with really funny eyes," said his mom.

Splat thought for a moment.
"But I haven't got eight legs," he replied.
"If you had, maybe you'd be a scary spider too?" teased his mom.
Splat made a scary-spider face.

Splat's mom caught the spider under a glass jar.
Splat looked closely at the spider. It didn't look
so scary now that it was trapped.

"Can I take the spider to school for Halloween?" asked Splat. "We've all made jack-o'-lanterns and everyone is dressing up in costumes and Mrs. Wimpydimple is going to tell a ghost story and there's a prize for the scariest cat and I want to be the scariest cat!

"So please can I take the spider to school . . . P-L-E-A-S-E?" he added without taking a breath.

"Okay," said his mom.

"Where's your Halloween costume?" asked his mom.
Splat pulled a broom from the closet and sat astride it.

"Aha! Look at me. I'm a scary witch's cat," cried Splat, racing around the kitchen.
"You certainly are scary," said his mom.

Then disaster struck.

Splat tripped over his tail and with a CRACK!
the broom handle snapped in two.

His scary witch's cat costume was ruined.

"Now I've got nothing to wear!" Splat groaned.
Even Seymour couldn't console him.

Splat's mom had an idea.
She stuffed some old socks with scrunched-up
newspaper and tied them to Splat with string.
"There!" she said.

Splat looked in the mirror and jumped back with a squeal. "Ohhh . . . I scared myself," he said.

He looked again and this time he smiled.
"Look at me!" he cried, waving his sock legs.
"I'm a big, scary sock spider."

Splat placed his jack-o'-lantern and spider on his wagon and set off to school.

On the way, he met Spike dressed as a mummy
and Plank dressed as a skeleton.

"They're pretty scary," said Splat.
Seymour nodded and trembled a little.

"But I'm scarier," said Splat.
Splat made his scariest spider face and growled.

Grrrrrrr.

Spike and Plank didn't even blink.

Instead . . .

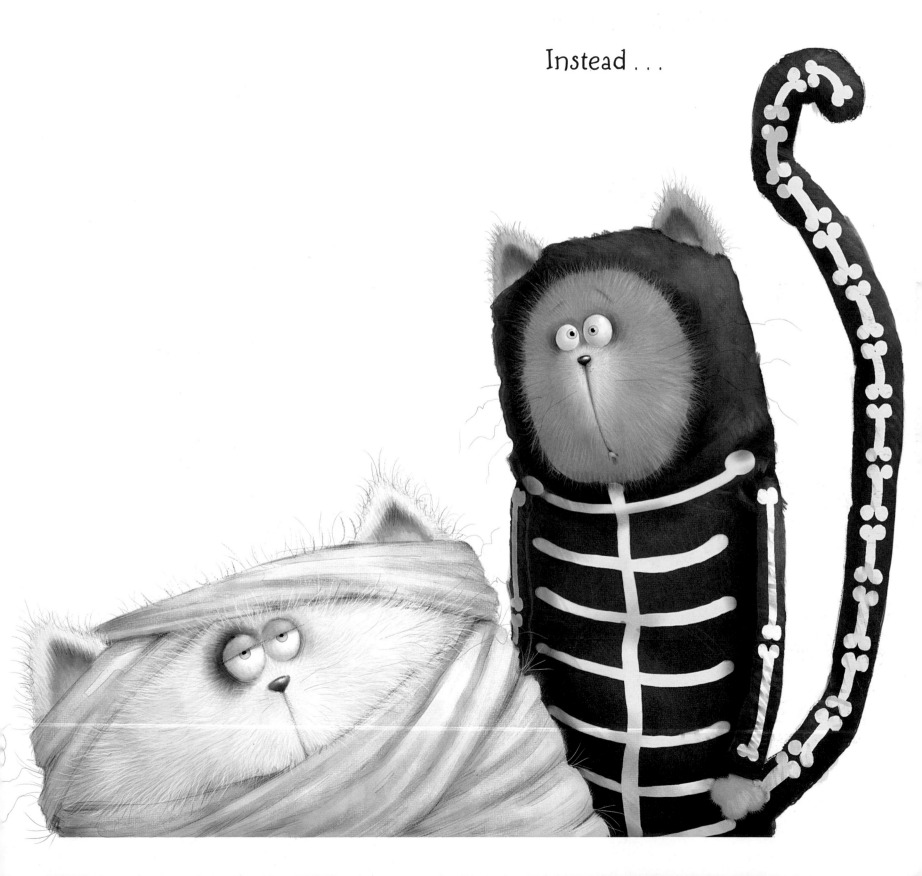

"BOO!" cried Spike.

"BOO!" cried Plank.

Splat yelped and jumped high in the air . . .

. . . and landed in a heap.

"Aww." Splat sighed. "Spike and Plank are both scarier than me."
Seymour nodded and trembled a little bit more.
"I'll never win the prize for scariest cat," said Splat.

The sock spider, the skeleton, and the mummy
continued on their way to school.

In class, everyone showed their jack-o'-lanterns.

Splat's jack-o'-lantern made everyone laugh.
"Awww." Splat sighed. "I'll never win the prize for scariest cat."
Seymour shook his head.

Everyone placed flashlights in their jack-o'-lanterns, and Mrs. Wimpydimple turned down the lights and whispered in her best ghost-story voice.

"In the dark, dark wood there's a dark, dark house.

In the dark, dark house there's a dark, dark room.

In the dark, dark room there's a dark, dark box . . .

and in the dark, dark box there's . . . a . . .

"...ghost!"

Mrs. Wimpydimple cried.

The class jumped with fright!

Splat was so startled, his tail whipped around and sent his jack-o'-lantern spinning through the air. And what goes up must come down.

SPLAT!

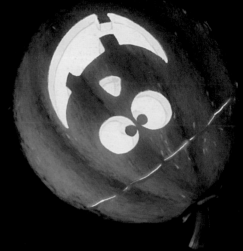

Unable to see anything, Splat stumbled around the classroom.

Everyone shrieked as the pumpkin head glared at them and made strange **whoo-whoo**-ing noises.

Whhhhhooooooooooooooooooooooo

Mrs. Wimpydimple turned on the lights and lifted up the wayward jack-o'-lantern.

The shrieking turned to laughter as Splat fell out.

"Calm down, calm down," hushed Mrs. Wimpydimple. "Now, class, who should win the prize for being the scariest cat?"

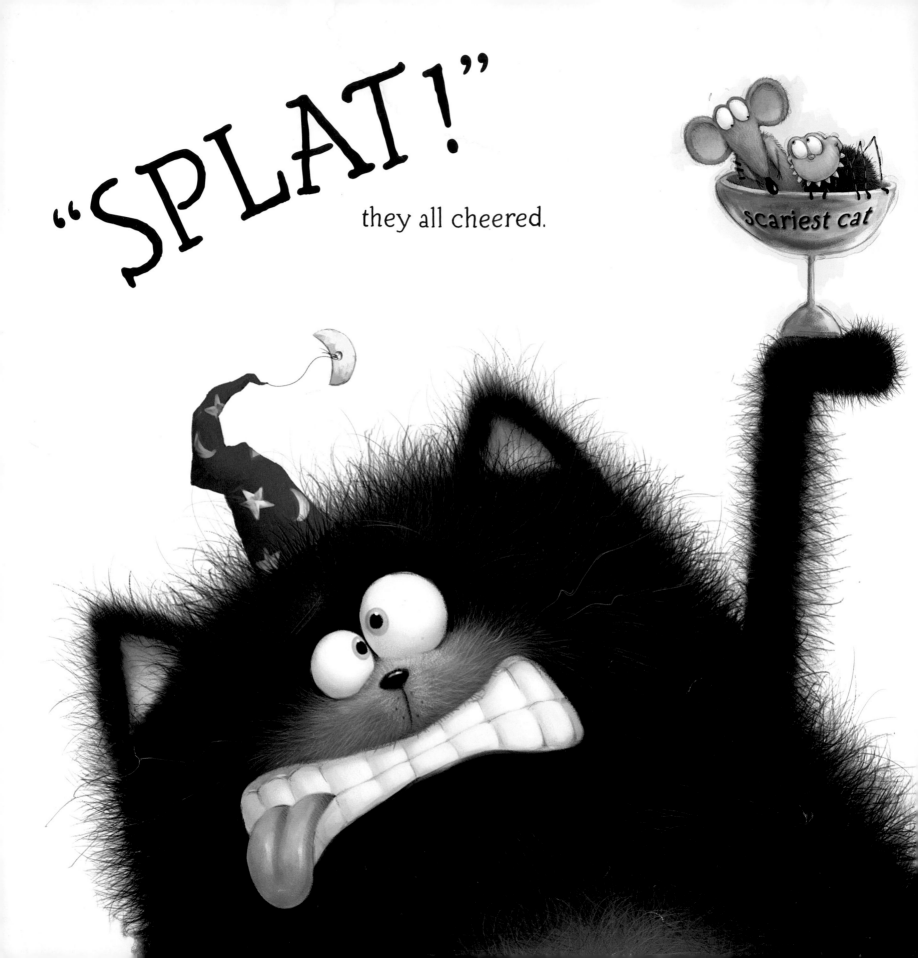

"SPLAT!" they all cheered.